LEROY
AND THE
TURNIP GREEN
PATCH

WRITTEN BY: LADELL BEAMON
ILLUSTRATED BY: AARON LIDDELL

ARPress
45 Dan Road Suite 36
Canton MA 02021

Hotline: 1(888) 821-0229
Fax: 1(508) 545-7580

Ordering Information:
Quantity Sales. Special discounts are available on quantity purchases by corporations, associations, and others. For details, contact the publisher at the address above.

Printed in the United States of America.

ISBN-13   Softcover   979-8-89356-796-0
                       eBook   978-1-64961-967-9

Library of Congress Control Number: 2021922322

With only $200.00 left to her name, she spent most of her days buying lottery tickets in hopes of winning the lottery. Leroy would watch his mother spend their last money on lottery tickets in hopes that she would win enough money to get them out of the lifestyle that they were living in.

One day when Leroy was on his way to school, he bumped into Jack Legged John, the neighborhood conman. Jack Legged John could con the freckles off a strawberry. He was so good until one day he sold his momma her own car for $600.00 and she never knew it was her car. Now, Leroy knew how tricky Jack Legged John could be so he tried to avoid talking to him, but Jack Legged John refused to leave Leroy alone until he listened to what he was trying to sell him.

"Alright John, you got 2 minutes cause I got to get to school and I am not about to let you con me into buying something that I don't need", said Leroy. John was so clever until he began to con Leroy by turning around and walking off

"Okay Leroy, it doesn1t matter any way. You will never get the secret to getting money now. So it is what it is", said Jack Legged John. It was too late for Leroy to avoid John because Leroy was nosey and loved to hear secrets so much until he stopped John in his tracks and started to ask about the secrets to getting money. Jack Legged John convinced Leroy to give him $2 for some magical turnip green seeds.

He told Leroy that overnight a magical turnip green plant would grow if he watered it after dark. He told Leroy that a giant stayed at the top of the turnip green patch beyond the clouds and possessed a magical lottery ticket. He filled Leroy's head with ideas of flying radios and chocolate covered ham hocks. This made Leroy very curious, but all he really thought about was his mother and the magical lottery ticket. So thinking about his mother, he did what a boy that loves his mother would do. He gave up his lunch money for the magical seeds and trotted off to school.

Leroy watched the dock quickly go from 8:30 a.m. to 2:12 p.m. He was so excited until as soon as he heard the bell ring, he took off. On his way home Leroy bumped into Hansello and Gertrude that were headed to Mom and Pop's corner store. He told them about his magical seeds that he got from Jack Legged John who most people call the Mysterious Hustler. This really got Hansello and Gertrude excited because Leroy was in such a rush to get home to tell his mom.

Mom's

Leroy got home from school and couldn't wait to tell his mother about his magical seeds. He jumped up and down and got very excited while he was talking to his mother. She told him, "Leroy calm down before you drive a hole in the floor. Now, what is it?" Leroy told his mom that he brought some magical seeds with his lunch money and wanted to plant the seeds so he could climb up into the magical turnip green patch and bring her home the magical lottery ticket and some chocolate ham hocks to go along with the huge bunches of greens that they would be eating forever. Leroy waited for his mom to get excited with him, but instead, she was so angry until she screamed at Leroy from the top of her lungs. She told him that he just got pranked and should have been waiting for the cameras from the Reality Show "Punked" to come out and show the world what a fool he was.

She quickly grabbed the seeds from him, threw them out of the window and told him to go up his room and go to bed.

Leroy was so sad that he went right up to his room, opened his window and started crying. Leroy's tears fell on the magical seeds. Leroy cried himself to sleep in the window and started sucking his thumb.

Four hours had passed, and Leroy was in total shock at what he was seeing before his very eyes. Now we don't know if it was the ears from Leroy's eyes or the slob from sucking his thumb, but one thing for sure is that someone watered the seeds that grew the magical turnip green patch that extended all the way up into
the clouds. This was amazing!.

This pigeon was from the hood because he had on a scarf and some Jordan's. The huge pigeon flew up to the top of the Giant Turnip Green Patch and dropped Leroy off on a leaf.

From a distance, Leroy saw a huge Night Club ahead of him with Neon Lights that said, "No Short People Allowed." Leroy quickly ignored the sign and ran towards the Night Club. He heard loud music and laughter that sounded like thunder roaring. He knew that it was the giant. Leroy got himself ready to do battle with the giant.

NO SHORT PEOPLE
ALLOWED

You would have thought that a million people was in this club, but it was just the Giant, a pile of chicken bones, a giant bottle of hot sauce and the giant's loud television set that he kept flipping back and forward from BET videos, back to the lottery drawing. Leroy fixed his eyes on this golden ticket that the Giant held in his hand.

Now Leroy had climbed all the way up to the Giant 1s window to peep
in because a huge dog with a tuxedo on and a pink beret on his head
kept watch at the velvet rope that guarded the door to the club. It was
easier to go through the window because that huge dog might have had
some funny business going on.

Leroy was almost through the crack in the huge window until he heard this loud music coming towards him getting closer and closer. He looked over his shoulder only to see a huge flying radio that was playing Pumps and a Bump by MC Hammer. Leroy ducked and the flying radio crashed through the Gi ant's window. The Giant jumped up because he was startled at the crash. Now pay attention to this next part because you won't believe what happened next.

The flying radio dips Leroy by his shirt on the way down crashing through the window. The Giant's pants were sagging when he jumped up because he watched too many BET videos and he thought it was the style. Because of his pants sagging , Leroy and the crashing flying radio fell down into the crack of the Giants pants. Leroy smelled a foul odor coming from the Giant because he had been sitting up for so long waiting for the lottery ticket number to be called that he forgot to take a bath. Because of the smell, Leroy grabbed a bottle of Odor Ban and began spraying in the Giant's pants.

This caused the Giant to start hopping and jumping, shaking his leg.

The Giant's pants finally fell to his ankles as Leroy and the flying radio came out of his pants. All the shaking caused the music to change to this song called The Stanky Legg as Leroy grabbed the magical lottery ticket that the Giant had dropped while being startled by the radio and Leroy crashing through the window.

Leroy takes off running with the ticket as the Giant gets angry and begins to run after him. Fee Fi Foe Fum, I 'm getting ready to get this little bum said the Giant. At that point, Leroy is so scared until he runs past the dog with the tuxedo on and the pink beret. The dog never even bothers to stop Leroy because he is too busy doing the Stanky Legg.

The Giant trips up and falls down again because of his sagging pants. This fall starts a huge earthquake that creates a huge blast of wind sending Leroy through the clouds and the turnip green patch. While falling through the clouds, the giant pigeon catches Leroy and takes him safety home.

Climbing back into his window, Leroy gives the Pigeon some of the crackers that were on his nightstand. The Pigeon turned down the crackers and said, "no thanks little homie, I just wanted to make sure that you were straight." With two big flaps, the Giant Pigeon flew back up into the clouds dropping Giant Pigeon droppings saying, "Excuse me, it1s been a long day."

Leroy couldn't wait to tell his mom what had happened, so he quickly ran down the steps to discover his mother crying and praying while the television set was tuned into the lottery channel. Leroy listened to his mother crying and praying. She never noticed that Leroy was standing behind her. In this magical moment, the lottery ticket begins to glow as the winningnumbers to the lottery were being called out on television. Leroy looked at the ticket only to realize that they had just won the lottery of 15 million dollars. Leroy turned around, walked up to his mother and shook her. He told her that she had just won the lottery. Leroy's mother wiped her eyes and looked at this Giant ticket and started screaming for joy.

She quickly hugged Leroy and begins to ask questions. Leroy looked at his mom and said I love you and you would n1t believe me if I told you. Let's just get out the hood.

The End!

Heal The Hood Foundation Of Memphis
Presents
A HOOD FABLE
LIL RED
Coming Soon to a hood
near you.....